Tamara Einstein &
Einstein Sisters

KidsWorld

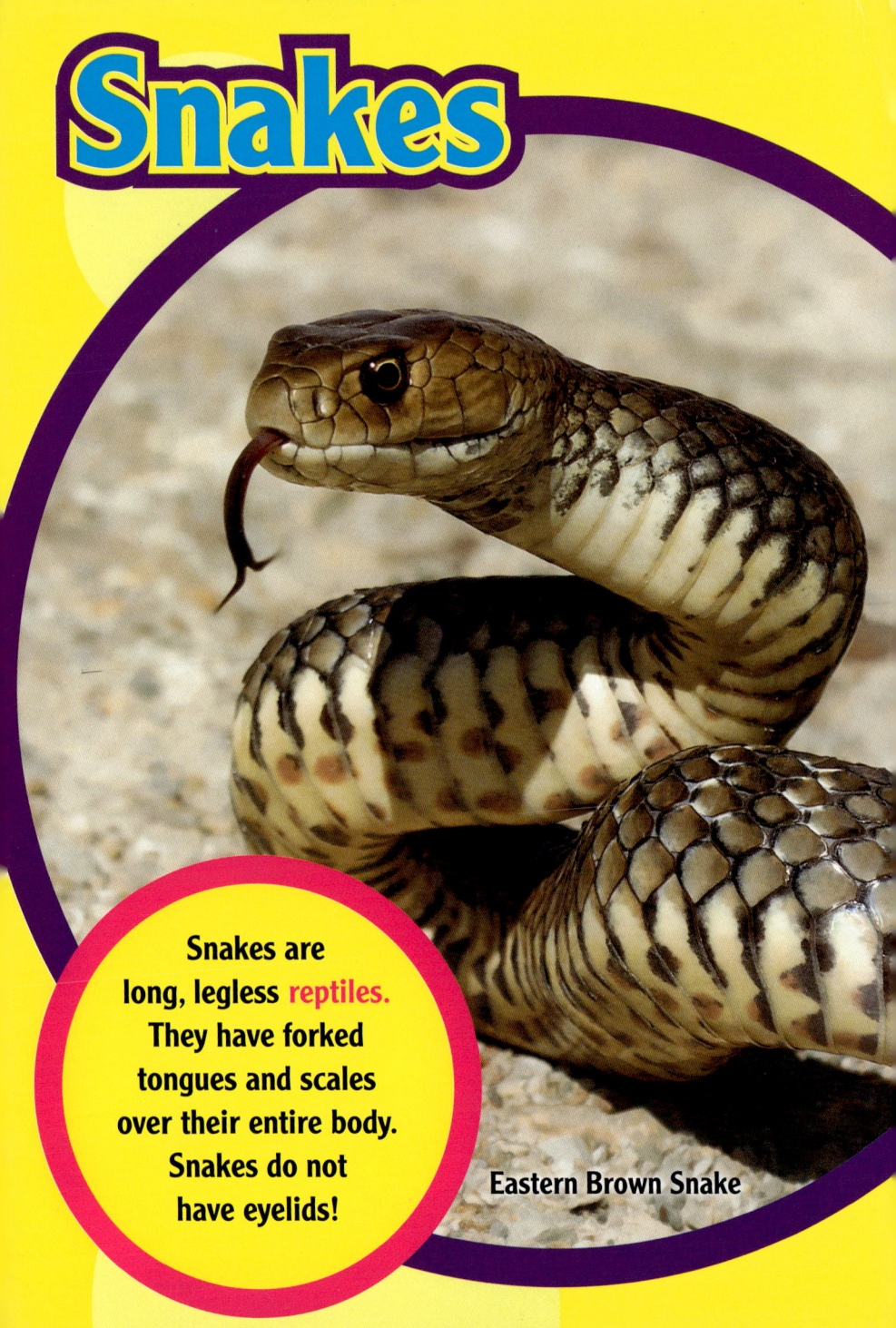

# Snakes

Snakes are long, legless reptiles. They have forked tongues and scales over their entire body. Snakes do not have eyelids!

**Eastern Brown Snake**

Snakes are often said to be just heads and tails. Snakes actually have elongated bodies and very short tails!

King Cobra

Many people are afraid of snakes. Not all snakes are venomous, and only some of the venomous ones are deadly. Most snakes pose no risk to people.

# Reptiles

**Reptiles** are **cold-blooded** animals. This means their body temperature changes as the air temperature changes. Reptiles also have four legs or have ancestors with four legs. All snakes have four-legged ancestors.

Painted Turtle

Reptiles include turtles, crocodiles, lizards and snakes. Dinosaurs were reptiles too!

Nile Crocodile

Most reptiles lay eggs. Reptiles are mainly **carnivorous,** meaning they eat other animals to survive.

Eastern Collared Lizard

# Anatomy

Snakes have long bodies. They have more bones in their backs—called **vertebrae**—than any other creature. Some snakes may have several hundred vertebrae! They also have many pairs of ribs.

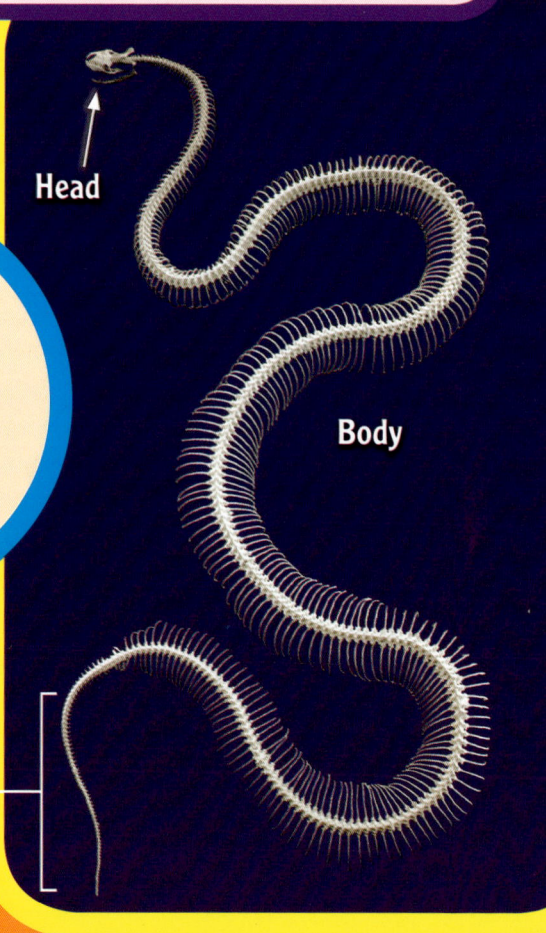

Head

Body

Tail

Snakes have short tails compared to the length of their bodies.

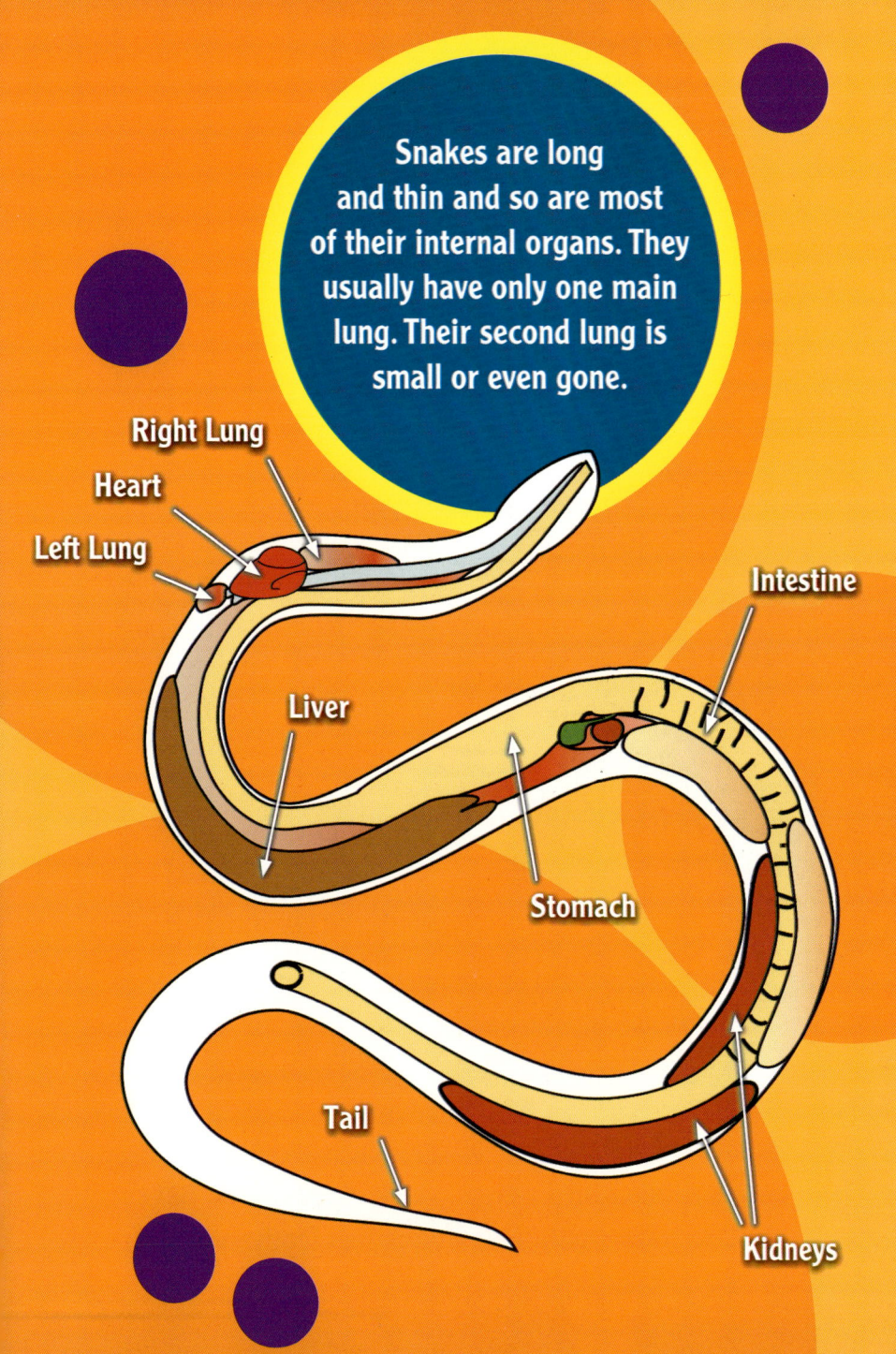

# Eggs

Snake Eggs

Most snakes lay **eggs.** Snake eggs are shaped like ovals. Unlike bird's eggs, snake eggs do not have a hard shell. Snake eggs feel leathery.

Hatching Pythons

Newly Hatched Snakelet

A baby snake is called a snakelet. When snakelets hatch they are fully-formed and able to move, eat and drink.

# Nests

Pine Snake Eggs

Most snakes lay eggs in a warm place, or they bury them in loose soil or sand. After laying eggs, the female usually leaves the eggs.

King Cobra

Only two kinds of snakes are known to make real nests. The king cobra makes a pile of leaves and grass in which the female lays her eggs.

Grass Snake Nest

Female grass snakes lay their eggs in rotting vegetation. The decomposition (rotting) provides heat to help the eggs develop.

# Protecting Eggs

Female Python Protecting Eggs

**Pythons** are the only snakes that protect their eggs. Females coil around their eggs to keep them safe. Sometimes the female will shiver to create a bit of heat to help the eggs develop.

Some females wrap themselves around their eggs so well that the eggs don't even touch the ground.

Female pythons stay coiled around their eggs until they hatch—about 55 days! They may leave their eggs only once in a while to drink or bask in the sun. Pythons can go for long periods without eating.

# Live Birth

Rattlesnake with Young

Some female snakes, such as rattlesnakes, keep their eggs inside their bodies until they hatch. A female rattlesnake may even stay with her snakelets for several weeks to ensure their safety.

Green Anaconda

Green anacondas and boa constrictors are unique among snakes. Their young develop as embryos inside the female's body but not inside an egg. When the embryos have fully developed, the female gives birth.

Boa Constrictor Snakelet

# Hibernating

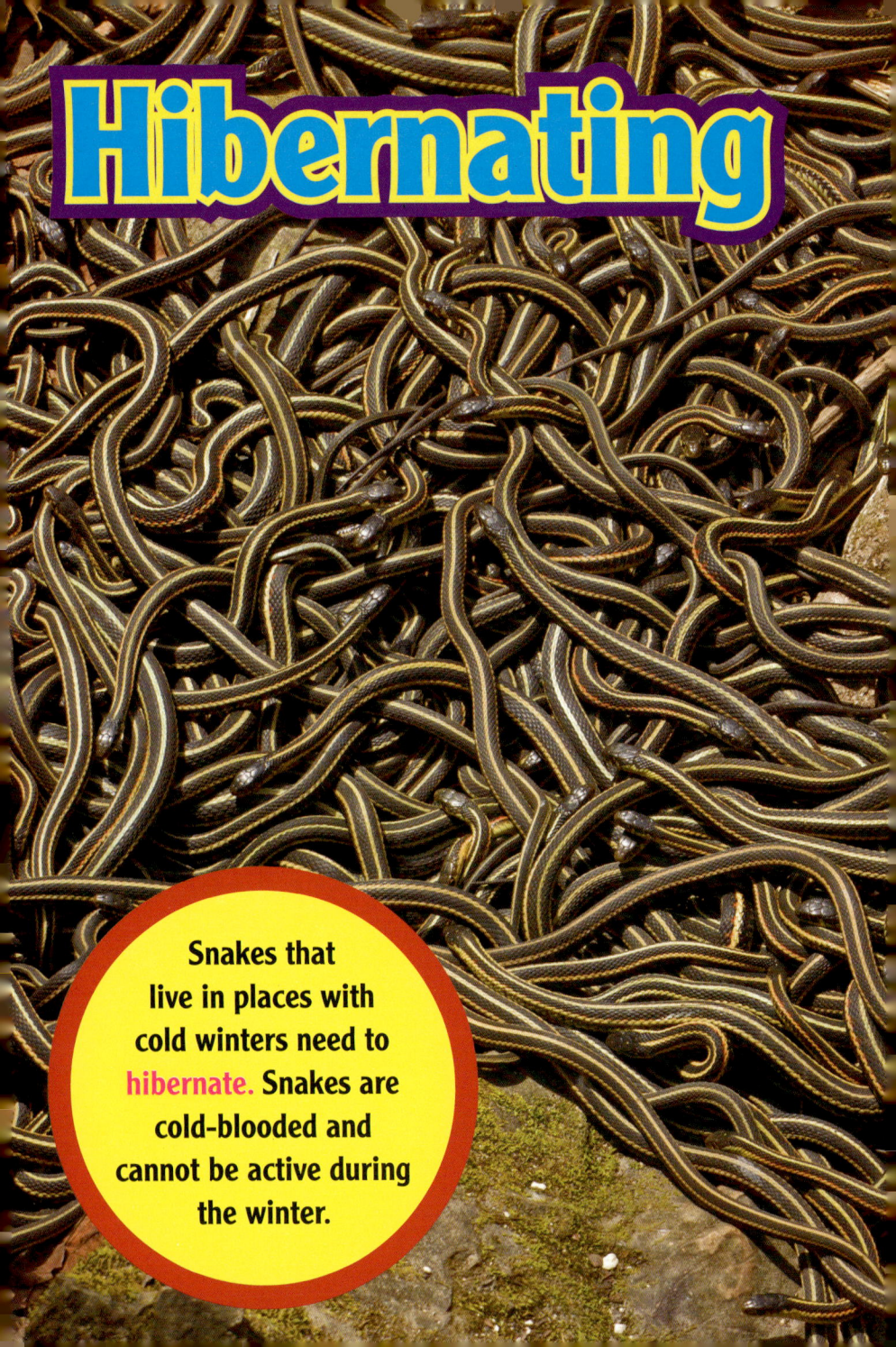

Snakes that live in places with cold winters need to **hibernate.** Snakes are cold-blooded and cannot be active during the winter.

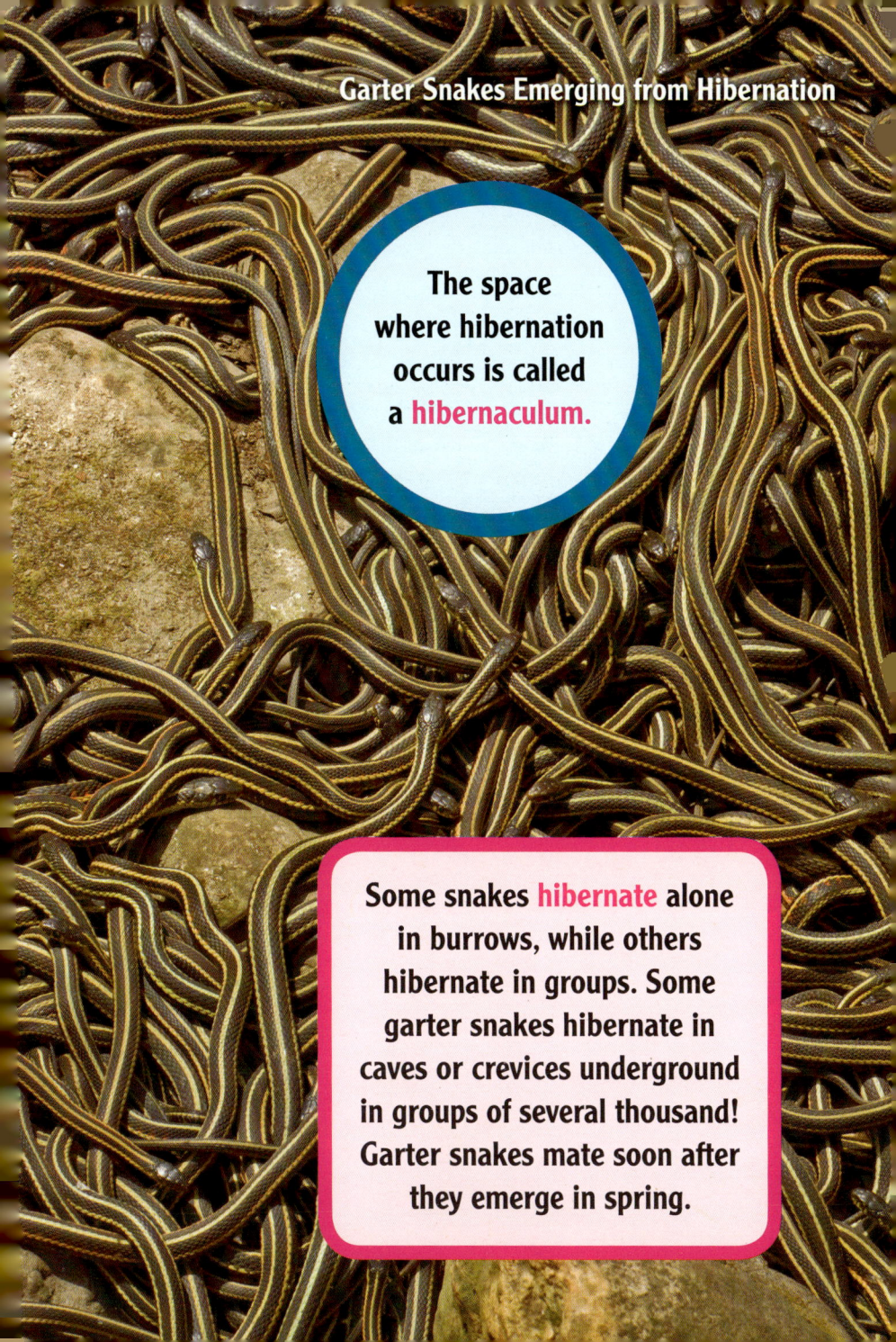

**Garter Snakes Emerging from Hibernation**

The space where hibernation occurs is called a **hibernaculum.**

Some snakes **hibernate** alone in burrows, while others hibernate in groups. Some garter snakes hibernate in caves or crevices underground in groups of several thousand! Garter snakes mate soon after they emerge in spring.

# Movement

**Green Whip Snake**

Snakes mainly move using a *slithering motion.* They move side to side and push against ridges or objects on the ground to slide forward. This is also how snakes move in water.

**Eastern Garter Snake**

Golden Tree Snake

Snakes are good climbers. They have strong muscles throughout their body that help them push against the bumps on tree bark so they can climb. They can also slither and climb on and around tree branches.

Sidewinder Rattlesnake

**Sidewinding** is used by a few species of snake, particularly the **sidewinder rattlesnake** in southern North America. Sidewinding is used on sand or slippery mud where objects or ridges to push against are rare. To sidewind, the snake lifts some parts of its body up and forward while supporting itself with the other parts on the ground. Sidewinding leaves a unique track on the ground.

# Flying Snakes

Strange but true, some snakes can fly!

Paradise Flying Snake

They don't fly in the same way as birds do, but five species of snakes can flatten their bodies and glide through the air. They can glide for about 100 meters (330 feet). That's about as long as a soccer field!

Golden Tree Snake

A flying snake climbs to the top of a tree and then out onto a branch. From there it launches itself into the air.

Flying snakes eat geckos and other lizards, as well as bats and some birds.

Golden Tree Snake Eating a Gecko

Some snakes live near water and can swim with ease. The largest snake, the **green anaconda,** spends more time in the water than out. It is also much faster when swimming than when moving on land.

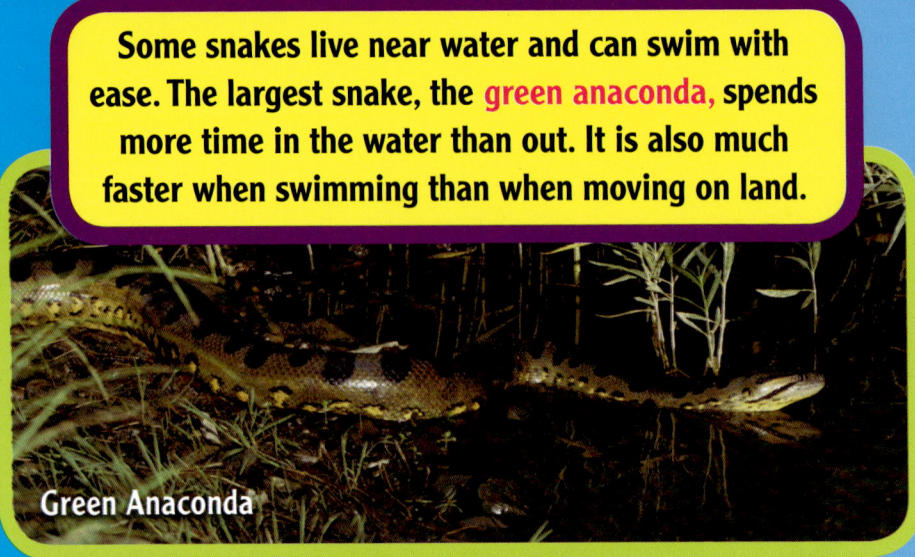

Green Anaconda

Dice Snake

**Dice snakes** and **garter snakes** enter water to hunt small fish and to escape larger predators.

Garter Snake

**Sea snakes** spend their entire lives underwater in seas and oceans. The tail is flattened sideways to act like paddle. They do not have gills and must come to the surface to breathe.

Banded Sea Krait

# Swimming

# Sleeping

**Green Tree Python**

Snakes do not have any eyelids, so if can be hard to tell if they're asleep! If a snake is coiled up and looks like it is resting, it is likely asleep. **Green tree pythons** tend to drape themselves over large branches to sleep.

Red-bellied Black Snake

**Snakes have transparent scales over their eyes, so even though they don't have eyelids, their eyes are protected from damage or drying out while they sleep.**

Carpet Python

# Eyes

Green Tree Snake

Some snakes, especially those that live in caves or burrows, have poor eyesight. Most snakes, however, have good vision. Snakes that live in trees and hunt fast-moving lizards and birds have the best vision.

Snakes lack eyelids. Instead, they have protective transparent scales over each eye, called **brilles**.

Shed Skin with Brilles

Grass Snake—Diurnal

Snakes with slit pupils tend to be nocturnal, that is they are active at night. Snakes with round pupils are diurnal, meaning they are active during the day.

Emerald Tree Boa—Nocturnal

# Heat Sensors

Pit vipers, pythons and some boas have special holes between their nostrils and eyes. These are called **labial pits.** The pits allow the snake to sense the heat from warm-bodied animals such as mice. Even if they cannot see or smell, the snake can still sense the heat from its prey and accurately strike at it.

Labial Pits

Western Diamondback Rattlesnake

Green Whip Snake

Snakes do not have external ears. They do have internal ear structures that connect to their jaw bone. By placing their jaw on the ground or branch they can hear the vibrations made by their prey.

Snake Skull

Lower Jaw Bone

# Hearing

# Skin

A snake's skin is covered with scales. Its skin is dry to the touch, not slimy. Snakes can have skin in a variety of colors and patterns. Their color patterns help with camouflage and hunting.

Rattlesnake Scales

California Mountain Kingsnake

Once in a while, a snake must shed its old skin. Shedding its skin allows a snake to grow and remove external parasites. They may soak in water and rub their bodies on rocks and twigs to help pull off the old skin.

Shed Skin

The shed skin usually comes off in one piece and inside-out, like pulling off a pair of tight, wet jeans.

Prairie Rattlesnake

Snakes have long, **forked tongues.** Their tongues flick in and out of their mouths very quickly. They don't have many taste buds on their tongue, so their sense of taste is not good.

# Taste and Smell

**Western Rat Snake**

A snake's tongue is used for smelling. Each fork of the tongue takes samples of particles in the air or on the ground and transfers them to a special "smelling" organ in the snake's mouth.

**Green Pit Viper**

Even though snakes have nostrils, their sense of smell in their nose is poor. To really "smell" their surroundings, they use their tongue!

# Fangs

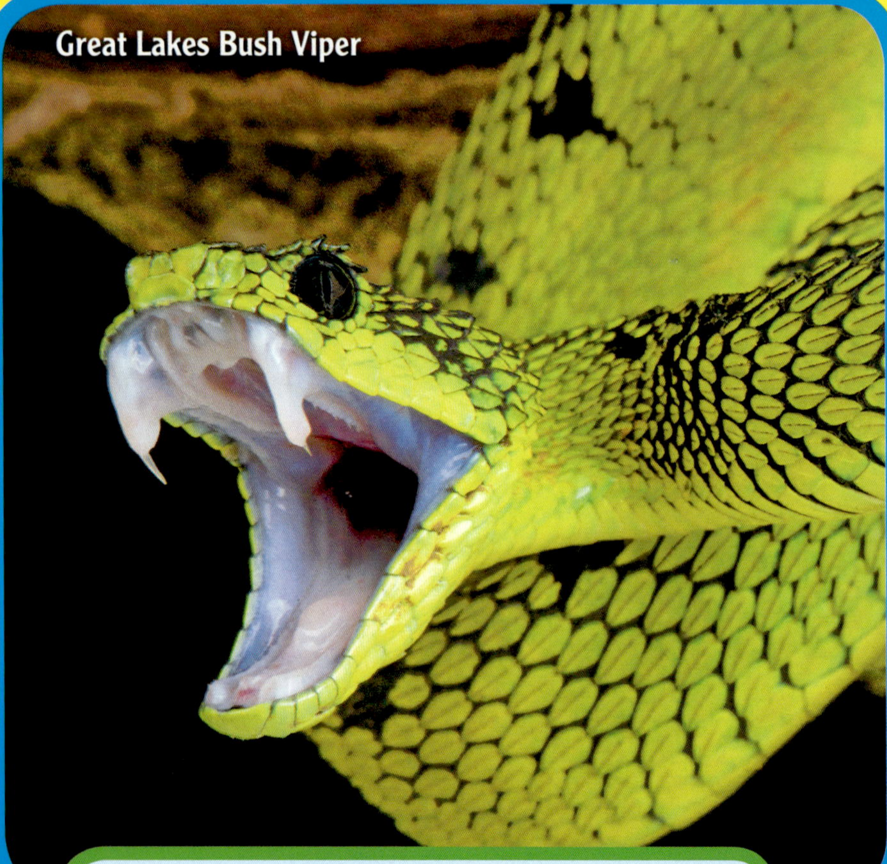

Great Lakes Bush Viper

Many snakes have large, sharp **fangs.** Fangs are used to inject **venom** into prey. Not all snakes have such big fangs. Some snakes have small fangs, and a few don't have any at all!

Snakes have other teeth too! Their smaller teeth resemble fangs, but do not have venom. Their teeth grasp their prey as they move their jaws over it.

Rattlesnake Fangs

Some snakes have fangs that rotate forward when the snake opens its mouth. This makes it easier for the snake to bite and inject venom into its prey.

# Venom

**Spitting Cobra**

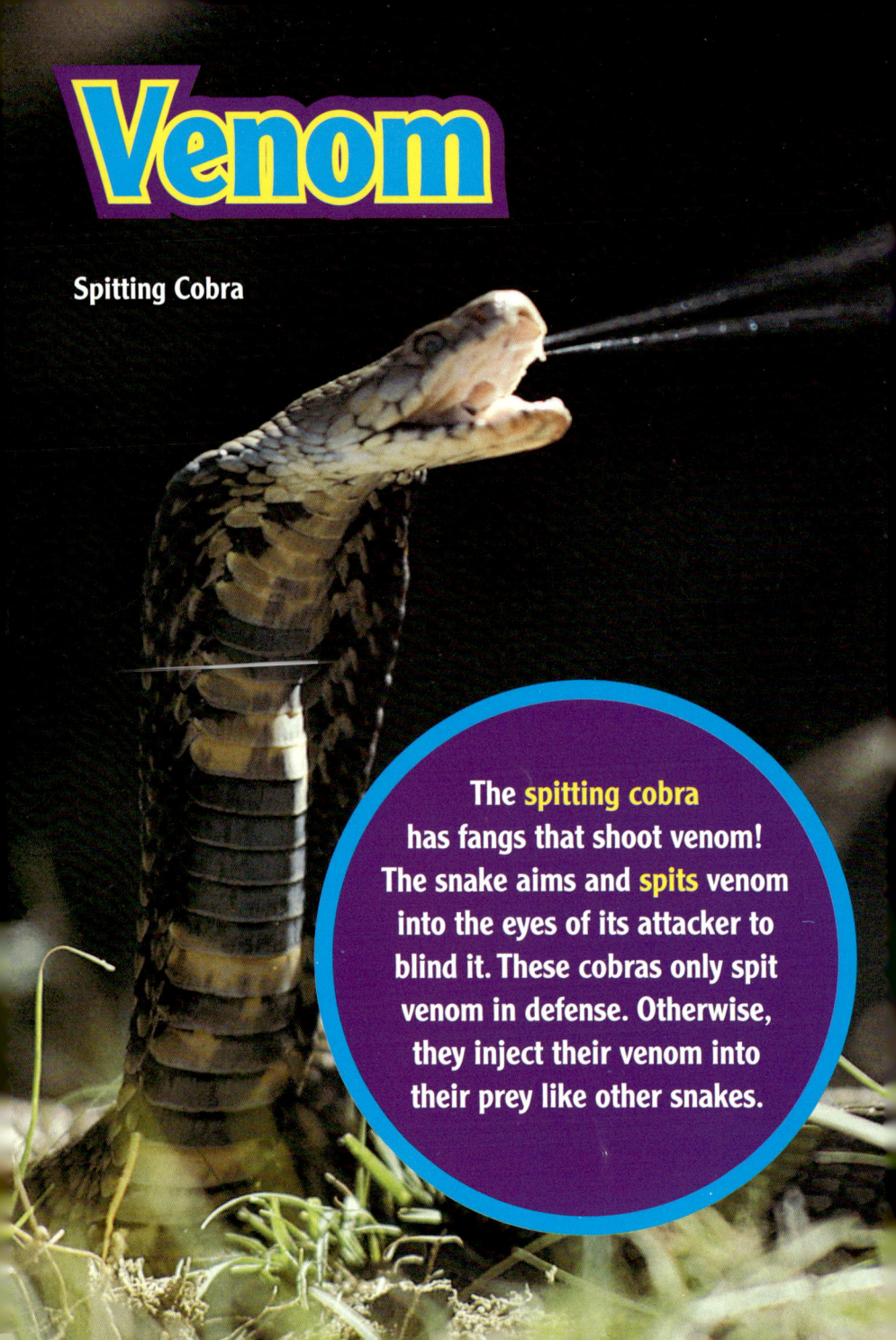

The **spitting cobra** has fangs that shoot venom! The snake aims and **spits** venom into the eyes of its attacker to blind it. These cobras only spit venom in defense. Otherwise, they inject their venom into their prey like other snakes.

Snake venom is actually saliva! Venom is a mix of special proteins that is stored in glands at the back of the head. Different snakes have different kinds of venom. A snake's venom is specially suited for killing its preferred prey.

Milking venom

Venom kills either by paralyzing the prey or by stopping its heart.

Antivenin is a medicine made from venom and is used to treat snake bites. Scientists get venom from a snake by "milking" its fangs.

# Constriction

Some snakes use **constriction** to kill their prey instead of venom. Snakes that do this are called **constrictors**.

Gray-banded Kingsnake

Golden Tree Snake

Man Demonstrating the Strength of a Python

Scientists have shown that constriction kills by cutting off the circulation of blood, not by suffocation.

Large constrictors, such as the reticulated python, are strong enough to kill a human. It can take two people to unwind a large constrictor from a person.

# Hunting

Many snakes are **ambush hunters.** They wait motionless for animals to come into striking range.

**White-lipped Pit Viper Ready to Strike**

**Spider-tailed Horned Viper**

The tip of the tail on a **spider-tailed horned viper** has modified scales to resemble a spider. The snake wiggles its tail to attract birds. When a bird comes close, the snake strikes it and eats it.

**Green Pit Viper Robbing a Nest**

Some snakes are *active hunters.* They stalk and chase their prey. Some snakes seek out birds nests to eat fledgling birds. Other snakes hunt fish in lakes or rivers.

**Dice Snake Eating a Fish**

# Eating

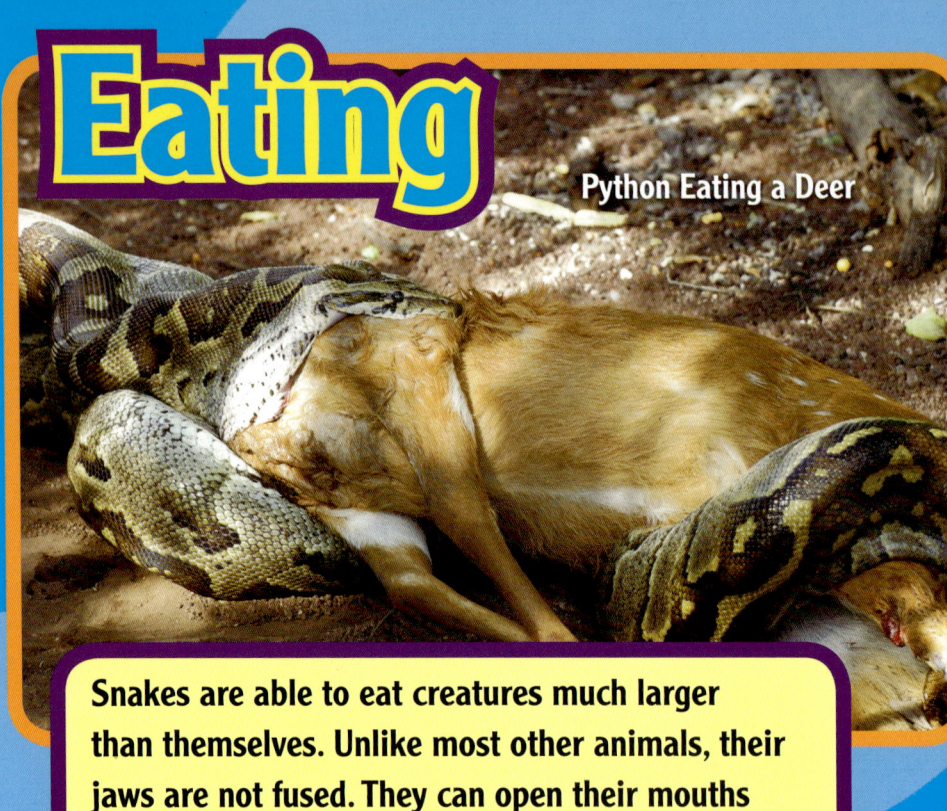

**Python Eating a Deer**

Snakes are able to eat creatures much larger than themselves. Unlike most other animals, their jaws are not fused. They can open their mouths extremely wide. They use their teeth to inch the whole body of their prey into their mouths.

**Golden Tree Snake Eating a Lizard**

**Bombay Earth Snake Eating a Worm**

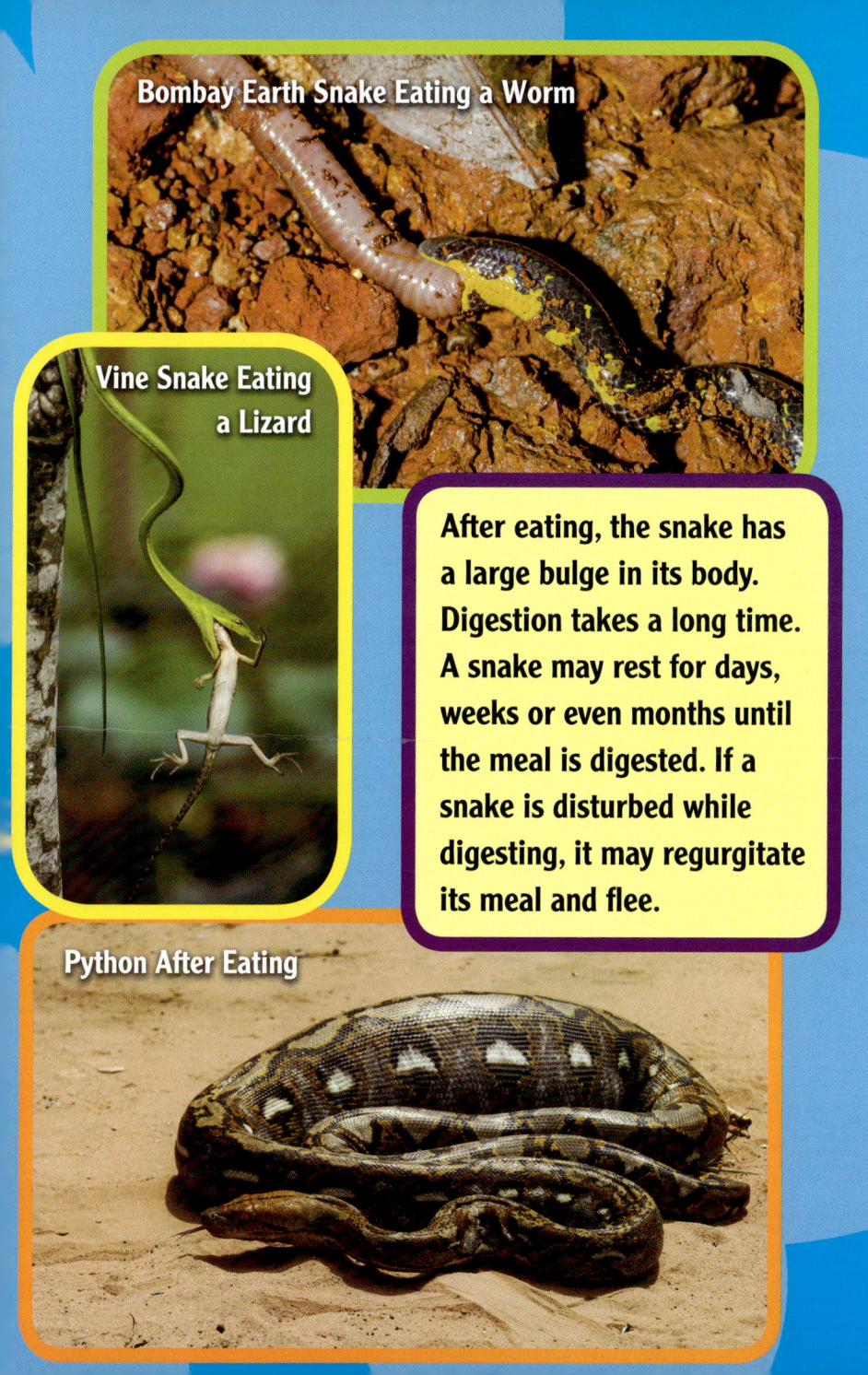

**Vine Snake Eating a Lizard**

After eating, the snake has a large bulge in its body. Digestion takes a long time. A snake may rest for days, weeks or even months until the meal is digested. If a snake is disturbed while digesting, it may regurgitate its meal and flee.

**Python After Eating**

# Egg Eaters

**Red-bellied Black Snake Eating Tree Snake Eggs**

Many kinds of snakes will eat eggs if they discover a nest. Snakes may eat the eggs of birds or other reptiles. Tiny thread snakes eat the eggs of ants and termites!

**Bullsnake Eating Mallard Eggs**

The **common egg-eating snake** of Africa is an egg-eating specialist. It feeds only on eggs. After swallowing an egg, special spines along the inside of its back break the egg. It then regurgitates the shell.

Common Egg-eating Snake

# Predation

**Indian Grey Mongoose**

Some animals, such as the mongoose, are immune to snake venom and can eat a variety of snakes, including cobras!

**Leopard**

**White Ibis**

Many birds and mammals prey on snakes. Some snakes also specialize in eating other snakes! The habit of eating snakes is called **ophiophagy**.

**Red Fox**

**Snake Eating a Snake**

# Defense

Rattlesnake

The **hollow rattle** on a rattlesnake's tail is made from **modified scales** that build up each time the snake sheds its skin. The snake shakes its tail to make a rattling sound. The sound is a warning to predatory animals that might be a threat to the rattlesnake.

Rattle

**Eastern Hognose Snake**

To avoid being eaten, the eastern hognose snake plays dead. It turns upside down and dangles its tongue out of its mouth. Many predators avoid eating dead things.

**Indian Cobra**

Cobras expand the skin of their necks when they are threatened. This makes them look bigger. Some cobras even have patterns on their necks that look like big eyes.

All snakes can hiss. It is like a general warning sound. Snakes prefer to save their venom for prey, so they'd rather scare away non-prey animals instead of biting them.

# Camouflage

**Dice Snake**

**Asp Viper**

Most snakes rely on camouflage to hide from predators. Camouflage is also useful while the snake is hunting.

**Saharan Horned Viper**

**Brown Vine Snake**

Snakes are usually camouflaged to look like the environment where they live. Some look like sand, others look like twigs and some snakes look like dead leaves.

**Gaboon Viper**

# Warning Colors

Coral Snake

Many animals that are venomous, poisonous or dangerous in some way have **warning colors.** Warning colors are often red or yellow. **Coral snakes** have bands of red and yellow, making it clear that they are dangerous and should be left alone!

**Blue Malayan Coral Snake**

Warning colors protect the snake from being harmed by a predator. They also protect the predator from harm by the snake.

**Banded Krait**

# Mimicry

**Sonoran Coral Snake**

**Eastern Coral Snake**

**Coral snakes** are dangerous venomous snakes that live in North America. Their warning colors protect them from many predators. **Mimicry** is when a non-dangerous creature looks like a dangerous one. Several non-venomous snakes mimic coral snakes so predators avoid them, too.

Venomous

# Non-venomous

**Scarlet Kingsnake**

Although they look like coral snakes, these snakes are not dangerous!

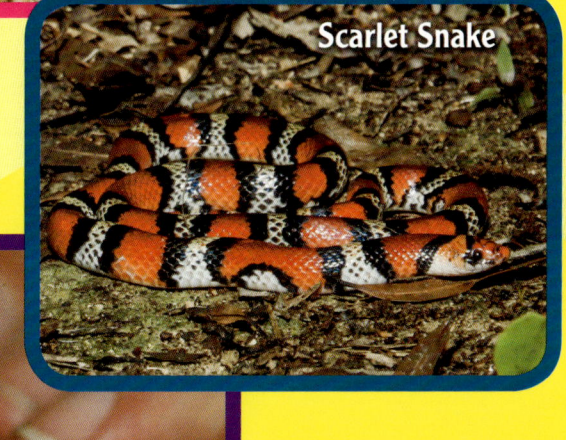

**Scarlet Snake**

**Western Shovelnose Snake**

**Arizona Mountain Kingsnake**

# Largest and Smallest

The green anaconda is considered the heaviest snake in the world with an average weight of about 100 kilograms (220 pounds). Some reports tell of green anacondas that are twice that weight!

Reticulated Python

The reticulated python is considered the longest snake at up to 10 meters (33 feet) long.

**Green Anaconda**

**Barbados Threadsnake**

**Brahminy Blind Snake**

The two **smallest** snakes in the world are the **Barbados threadsnake** and the **Brahminy blind snake.** Both live in soil and eat the eggs and larvae of ants and termites. They can both grow to 10 centimeters (4 inches long).

# When is a Snake not a Snake?

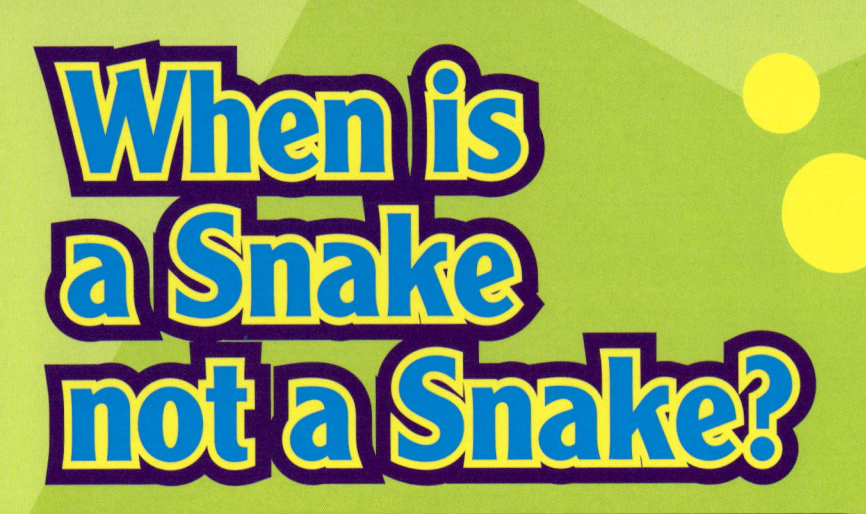

**Glass lizards** may look like snakes, but they are really legless lizards. Unlike snakes, lizards have external ears and eyelids. Lizards also do not have flexible jaws. They cannot eat things bigger than their heads.

Western Slender Glass Lizard

**Long-headed Caecilian**

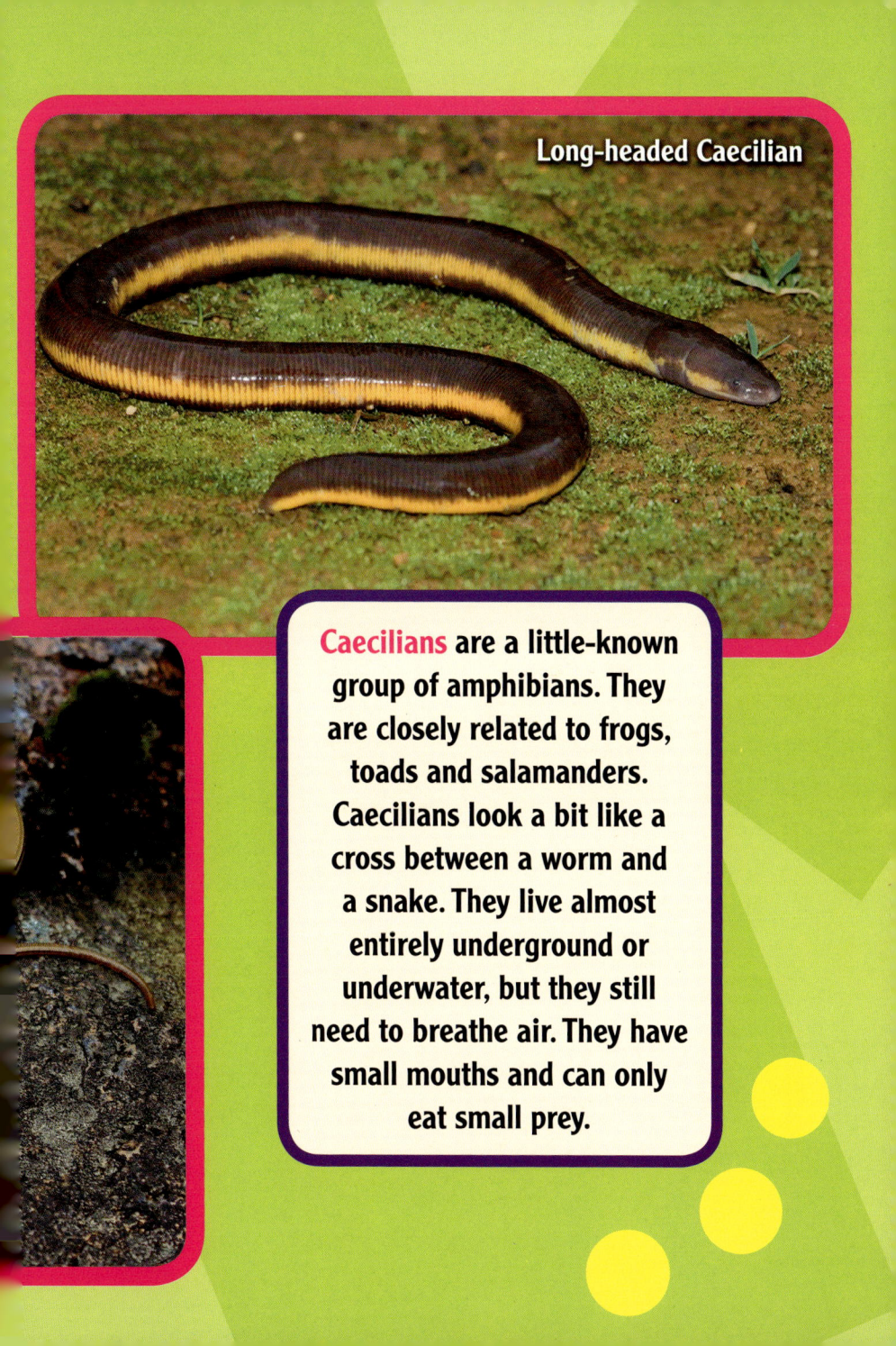

**Caecilians** are a little-known group of amphibians. They are closely related to frogs, toads and salamanders. Caecilians look a bit like a cross between a worm and a snake. They live almost entirely underground or underwater, but they still need to breathe air. They have small mouths and can only eat small prey.

# Problem Snakes

Burmese Python in Florida

**Burmese pythons** have become numerous in the Florida Everglades because as pets they were released into the wild. These invasive snakes have caused raccoon, opossum, bobcat, rabbit and fox numbers to decline.

**Brown Tree Snake**

The **brown tree snake** was accidentally introduced onto **Guam**, an island in the South Pacific. Without any natural predators, the population of these snakes grew rapidly and caused the decline of most small birds, mammals and reptiles on the island.

# Snakes in your Garden

**Garter snakes** are common throughout North America. They are slender snakes that are a welcome addition to a garden. They feed on slugs, bugs and small rodents that may damage plants and vegetables. Garter snakes are harmless to people.

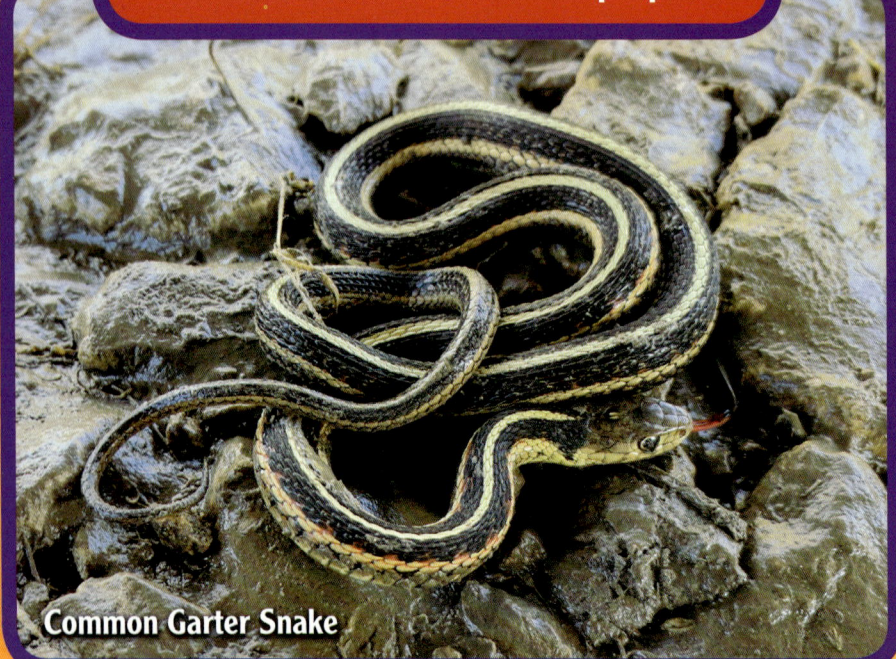

**Common Garter Snake**

Bullsnake

**Bullsnakes** and **gopher snakes** are not likely to live in a city garden, but they can be found in farmland. They can eat large number of rodents, such as gophers, that can damage crops and burrow into the cropland.

Scarlet Kingsnake

The **kingsnake** gets its name because it feeds on other snakes, making it the "king of snakes." There are five kinds of kingsnakes in North America. They can even eat rattlesnakes!

© 2018 KidsWorld Books
Printed in China

All rights reserved. No part of this work covered by the copyrights hereon may be reproduced or used in any form or by any means—graphic, electronic or mechanical—without the prior written permission of the publishers, except for reviewers, who may quote brief passages. Any request for photocopying, recording, taping or storage on information retrieval systems of any part of this work shall be directed in writing to the publisher.

The Publisher: KidsWorld Books

**Library and Archives Canada Cataloguing in Publication**

Title: Snakes / Tamara Einstein & Einstein Sisters.
Names: Einstein, Tamara, author. | Einstein Sisters, author.
Identifiers: Canadiana (print) 20190054077 | Canadiana (ebook) 20190054093 | ISBN 9781988183541 (softcover) | ISBN 9781988183558 (EPUB)
Subjects: LCSH: Snakes—Juvenile literature. | LCSH: Snakes—Miscellanea—Juvenile literature.
Classification: LCC QL666.O6 E46 2019 | DDC j597.96—dc23

*Front cover:* From Getty Images: Sunda Island Pit Viper, dekihendrik.

*Back cover:* Yellow Eyelash Viper *by* deputyrick, Getty Images; Indian Cobra by Pavan Kumar N, Wikimedia Commons; Great Lakes Bush Viper by reptiles4all, Getty Images.

*Photo credits:* From Getty Images: ABBPhoto 50b; amwu 56; AOosthuizen 47a; artiheart 22c; Artur Bogacki 9a; asxsoonxas 41a; BenGrasser 43b; bradwatsonphotography 49a; choan 47c; CUTWORLD 18a; Design Pics 51b; Digital Vision 36-37; dossly 47d; draskovic 6; ePhotocorp 53b; GracedByTheLight 5b; HRossD 32-33; hugocorzo 52; JasonOndreicka 55a, 55b; JEAN-FRANCOIS Manuel 46; JedsPics_com 42a; Jeremy Tomlinson 26a; John Foxx 37a; johnaudrey 48a; Juanmonino 35; juerpa 16-17; Jupiterimages 14; kasipat 30; Ken Griffiths 13a; kevdog818 55c; KristianBell 2; Leamus 50a; Lensalot 43a; maewjpho 21a; michaklootwijk 19b; mirceax 4; Noppharat05081977 8; oddonatta 19a; Panyawatt 3; passion4nature 47b; Rakib Islam 13b; reptiles4all 34; sakdinon 31b; serajace 23; shark_749 26b; Shoemcfly 33a; Sigrid61 27; Simona Tonoli 29a; SteveByland 28; taviphoto 22b, 51a; Thaisign 11a; thawats 39a, 42b; Thorsten Spoerlein 25b; tikephoto 21b; Tom Brakefield 22a, 49c; TommyIX 33b; USO 5a; Volodymyr Kucherenko 41b; vovashevchuk 24; Vu Vu 40a, 43b; Weber 54b. From Wikimedia Commons: born1945 31a; Dave Lonsdale 15a; David Jahn 54a; Davidvraju 57c; Dawson 9b; DestructiveEyes 15b; Georg Wilhelm 11b; Glenn Bartolotti 10, 63b; H. Krisp 51c, 55d; Hillebrand Steve, U.S. Fish and Wildlife Service 18b; JanRehschuh 57a; Jcraft75 38; Jud McCranie 48b; Mikeybear 25a; Mokele 29b; Mond76 45; Nicolas Perrault III 57b; Omid Mozaffari 40b; Pavan Kumar N 49b; Peter Paplanus 58; Psyon 63b; Ros Runciman 44a; Sandeep Das 59; Seshadri.K.S 53a; Soulgany101 61; Stephen Courtney 27a; Tigerpython 12; USFWS 60; USFWS Mountain-Prairie 44b; USFWSmidwest 62; Uwe Gille 7; vvar 39b. From Alamy: Cede Prudente 20-21.

We acknowledge the financial support of the Government of Canada.
Nous reconnaissons l'appui financier du gouvernement du Canada.

Funded by the Government of Canada | Canadä
Financé par le gouvernement du Canada

*PC:* 38